Fantail, Fantail

by Margaret Mahy

drawings by Bruce Phillips

Ready to Read

Learning Media
Wellington

"Fantail, Fantail,
have some cheese."

"No. No. No.
I don't like cheese."

"Fantail, Fantail,
have some peas."

"No. No. No.
I don't like peas."

"Fantail, Fantail,
have some pie."

"No. No. No.
I don't like pie."

"Fantail, Fantail,
have this fly."

"Yes. Yes. Yes.
I like that fly."

"I don't want cheese,
I don't want peas,
I don't want pie,

but I want that fly !"

"Goodbye, fly."